little monsters

To Aidan

little monsters +

Published by Doubleday
a division of Bantam Doubleday Dell Publishing Group, Inc.
666 Fifth Avenue, New York, New York 10103

Doubleday
and the portrayal of an anchor with a dolphin are trademarks of Doubleday,
a division of Bantam Doubleday Dell Publishing Group, Inc.

Originally published in Great Britain in 1989 by Orchard Books,
96 Leonard Street, London EC2A 4RH.

Library of Congress Cataloging-in-Publication Data applied for
ISBN 0-385-41343-2
Text and illustrations © Jan Pieńkowski 1989

Printed in Hong Kong
October 1990
First Edition in the United States of America

JAN PIEŃKOWSKI
Eggs for Tea

DOUBLEDAY

New York   London   Toronto   Sydney   Auckland

YUM
YUM

This
little
monster

can't
believe
his
eyes.

Six big eggs,
surprise surprise!

He gobbles one up

and

has

it

for

his

tea

GULP

and that leaves five
for you and me.

SMACK

This
little
monster

can't
believe
his
eyes.

Five big eggs,
surprise surprise!

He poaches one

SLURP

and
has
it
for
his
tea

and that leaves four
for you and me.

This
little
monster

can't
believe
his
eyes.

GLUG

Four big eggs,
surprise surprise!

z z z

He scrambles one

and
has
it
for
his
tea

and that leaves three
for you and me.

This
little
monster

can't
believe
his
eyes.

Three big eggs,
surprise surprise!

z z Z

He boils one

and
has
it
for
his
tea

and that leaves two
for you and me.

This
little
monster

can't
believe
his
eyes.

Two big eggs,
surprise surprise!

z z z

He fries one up

SIZZLE

and
has
it
for
his
tea

and that leaves one
for you and me.

z z Z

This little monster can't believe his eyes.

One egg left,
surprise surprise!

All gone!